BERNIE
and the Beast

Written by
SALLY KURJAN

Illustrated by
SHANNARA HARVEY

Bernie loved his home. He loved his new family, and especially loved playing outside with Spike.

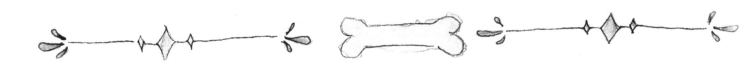

Every now and then, he would think
about his brothers and sisters
from his first home, but he knew
they had all found nice families too.

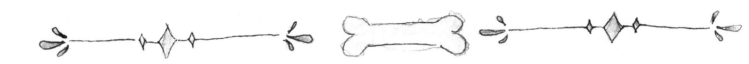

Bernie had lots of new friends. He and Spike played chase with the squirrel family. The squirrels were always faster and would run up the trees and laugh at the puppies.

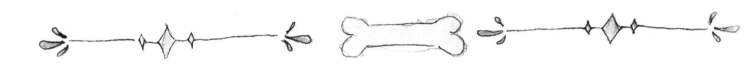

Bernie also loved his new neighbors.

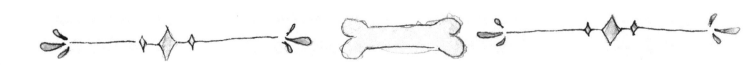

John and Sandy lived on one side
of his yard. John called Bernie
"Bernard" and that made Bernie
happy.

Little neighbors lived on the other side. Kaitlyn had long blonde hair and always said, "Hi Bernie!"

Drew ran up and down the fence, laughing when Bernie and Spike chased him.

Bernie couldn't see who lived behind his yard because there was a very tall wooden fence.

Sometimes the squirrels would run up and over the fence. Bernie could hear them playing, but couldn't see them until they climbed up a tree.

One day, Bernie and Spike were playing outside. All of a sudden they heard the loudest footsteps they had ever heard coming from the other side of the fence.

The puppies ran over to the fence to see
if they could tell what was making all
that noise.

Bernie and Spike were so frightened they ran back to their house as fast as they could!

Bernie was scared. He had never heard anyone make such loud sounds, so he was sure that it wasn't another puppy.

Then he realized what was on the other side of the fence.

It had to be a Beast!

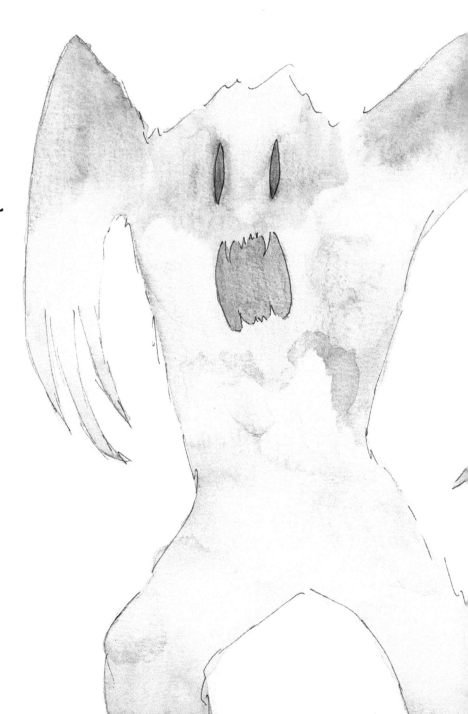

Every time Bernie and Spike went outside, they would listen for The Beast. Sometimes while they were playing, The Beast would stomp closely by the fence and bark very loudly. Bernie didn't like that at all.

Bernie thought to himself, "The Beast could knock the fence down and come into our yard!"

Bernie and Spike were very worried. They told each other, "Beasts are very large and very scary. They do not like to play with puppies. They might even bite!"

Ubu and Bella did not like The Beast either. They would run and hide whenever they heard him stomping around his yard.

One day Bernie heard a lady talking to The Beast. She called him "Phil" and told him that he was the smartest dog in the world!

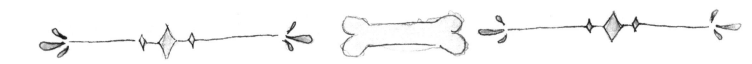

Bernie looked at Ubu and Bella and Spike. They couldn't believe it either! The Beast was a dog? And a smart one?

Then, the lady told Phil that he should meet his neighbors on the other side of the fence!

Bernie was so scared that he ran to his house as fast as he could. Bella and Spike and Ubu ran inside too. They did not want to meet The Beast Dog.

A little while later, the puppies were all taking a nap, and the doorbell rang.

They woke up when they heard
The Beast stomping into their house,
and he said "Hello" with the loudest
WOOF ever!

Phil towered over the puppies. He was the biggest dog any of them had ever seen!

Bella backed up to make sure Phil didn't smoosh her.

Bernie noticed that Phil's eyes were kind and he had a huge smile. Maybe The Beast would be a nice new friend!

"Let's go play," said Phil. The puppies were not too sure about that, but they all ran outside.

Phil dropped his toy in front of Bernie. He barked a big, happy WOOF when Bernie picked up the toy and ran. All of the puppies played and played until Bernie had to take a rest.

Bernie was so happy to have a new friend who loved to run and play ball. He was sorry he thought Phil was a beast.

From then on, Bernie and Spike couldn't wait to play with Phil. It was so much fun having a really big friend!

CPSIA information can be obtained
at www.ICGtesting.com
Printed in the USA
BVHW020213200419
546065BV00003B/7/P